# Girls to the Rescue
### BOOK #2

# Lion on the Prowl

## 10 inspiring stories
about clever and courageous
girls from around the world

*Edited by*
# Bruce Lansky

**Meadowbrook Press**

Distributed by Simon & Schuster
New York

**Library of Congress Cataloging-in-Publication Data**
Girls to the rescue: tales of clever, courageous girls from around
   the world/selected by Bruce Lansky.
      p. cm.
   MBP ISBN: 978-0-88166-251-1;  S&S ISBN: 978-1-442-49194-6
   1. Children's stories. [1. Short stories] I. Lansky, Bruce.
PZ5.G447   1995
[Fic]—dc20                                                                 95-17733

Editor: Bruce Lansky
Editorial Coordinator, Copy Editor: Liya Lev Oertel
Production Manager: Amy Unger
Cover Designer: Linda Norton
Production Coordinator: Danielle Dickey
Cover Illustration: Gay Holland

Published by
Meadowbrook Press
6110 Blue Circle Drive, Suite 237
Minnetonka, MN 55343

BOOK TRADE DISTRIBUTION by
Simon & Schuster, a division of Simon and Schuster, Inc.
1230 Avenue of the Americas
New York, NY 10020

18 17 16 15 14 13        20 19 18 17 16 15 14 13 12 11 10 9 8 7 6 5 4 3 2 1

Printed in the United States of America

# Dedication

This book is dedicated to my daughter, Dana. I used to make up stories for her when she was young, hoping to inspire her to believe in herself and to pursue her dreams. It is in that spirit that I have written and collected the stories in this series.

# Acknowledgments

Thank you to all the young women who served
on a reading panel for this project:

Laura Bohen, Connie Bottenberg, Kelly Bottenberg, Shekinah
Boyd, Valerie Breault, Bailey Campbell, Becky Carlson, Ashley
Collier, Katie Comstock, Courtney Davis, Megan Djerf,
Stephanie Djerf, Lisa Dosson, Emily Ederer, Amy Finnerty,
Lizzie Flannigan, Annie Fredrickson, Allison Garnett, Jill
Gotfredson, Katherine Graham, Carla Granger, Amanda
Griffin, Jennifer Lynn Gruenhagen, Jennifer Guptill, Asa Hall,
Jenifer Hamilton, Sydney Hanson, Haley Hastings, Catherine
Henderson, Kimberly Hicks, Katy Hinton, Allisun Holmes,
Elizabeth Holmes, Linda Hong, Becca Hoos, Vanessa Hoza,
Amy Jantz, Amanda Johnson, Jamie Judson, Jenney Kirby,
Christine Lamb, Hana Lee, Monica Lee, Leah Lehmkuhl,
Lauren Lieppman, Jessica Martin, Brittany Martinez, Kim
Mattern, Marijo Mendoza, Sydney Miniken, Nancy Muldor,
Britni Newton, Ashley Nobles, Amy Norris, Jennifer Owsiany,
Michelle Renee Panethiere, April Payne, Kelly Pendleton,
Amber Nicole Penrose, Amy Peterson, Stephanie Phillips,
Shelby Plaskanka, Lea Popkin, Cassie Powers, Cortney
Reihman, Kiera Reinsch, Claire Reuning, Melissa Roberts,
Julie Rogers, Amy Rossman, Layla Scott, Amy Seubert,
Michelle Verant, Kristen Webb, Rachael White,
Catherine Wicks, Hanna Zipes

# Contents

page

Cody's Wooden Whistle
*an original story by Douglas Dosson* .............................. 1

Adrianna's Chickens
*an original story by Anne Schraff* ..................................... 11

Liza and the Lost Letter
*an original story by Bruce Lansky*................................... 17

Jamila and the Lion
*an original story by Anne Schraff* .................................. 27

The Peacemakers
*an original story by Lois Greiman*................................... 35

Kim's Surprise Witness
*adapted by Bruce Lansky from a Chinese folktale* .............. 49

Vassilisa the Wise
*adapted by Joanne Mitchell from a Russian folktale*........... 59

Just a Girl
*an original story by Brenda Cox* .................................... 73

The Clever Daughter-in-Law
*adapted by Bruce Lansky from Chinese folklore*................. 81

Peggy's Magic Egg
*adapted by Stephen Mooser from an Irish folktale* .............. 93

Author Biographies ...........................................105

# Introduction

The response to the first *Girls to the Rescue* has been over-whelmingly positive, from girls, parents, teachers, booksellers, and reviewers. I have continued to write and search for new stories and we are trying to expand the series as fast as we can.

While I traveled around the country to bookstores, schools, and teacher conferences to talk about the first book, I had a number of interesting experiences that I'd like to share with you.

Often, adult women purchase *Girls to the Rescue* and say, "I never had a book like this when I was growing up. So, please inscribe this book to me." We all need "stories to live by," so don't be surprised if your teacher, aunt, or grandma wants to borrow your book.

I am no longer surprised when boys buy a copy of *Girls to Rescue* and ask me to inscribe it to them. Nor am I surprised when boys tell me that they've read one of the stories from their sister's book and liked it so much they finished the whole book. I am thrilled that boys like these stories too. Loan your book to your brother. Don't be surprised if he enjoys it, too.

I hope you like this book of stories as well as the first one.

Happy reading.

Bruce Lansky

# Cody's Wooden Whistle

## AN ORIGINAL STORY BY DOUGLAS DOSSON

Cody Richter sat on the feed box, carefully sanding her homemade wooden whistle. She held it up to the light of the barn's lantern burning just above her head. Since it was her very first try at whistle making, the shape was far from perfect. Cody put the whistle to her lips and blew hard.

"Tweeeeeet!" the whistle trilled sharply, startling the horse in the stall in front of her. At least the whistle worked, even if it didn't look so great.

Cody got up and walked over to the edge of the

stall. "Sorry I scared you, Ruby," she said to the spotted gray mare standing knee-deep in fresh straw.

This was the third night that Cody had sat outside Ruby's stall just waiting, killing time, and waiting some more. Ruby was about ready to deliver her first colt. Dad and Mom had promised that this colt would be Cody's.

With a grinding sound, the barn door behind Cody slid open. "Any luck yet?" a man's voice asked. It was Andy, one of the hired hands who helped break and train the horses on the Richter's ranch.

"No," Cody sighed. "It seems to be taking forever."

Andy took the lantern off the hook and very slowly stepped into the stall. As Cody watched anxiously, Andy carefully examined Ruby for signs that the birthing process was starting.

"You know, Cody," he said at last. "I could be wrong, but I think you'd better get your folks." With a joyful shout, Cody ran off into the darkness.

Andy was right. Within an hour Ruby was down. And with plenty of help from Mom and Dad, the new colt was born just before midnight. He was a beautiful little colt—all black except for some small white spots on his forehead.

Cody stayed with Ruby throughout the birth. She saw the new colt stand for the first time and she saw him take his first taste of mother's milk.

"What are you going to call him?" Dad asked, rolling down the sleeves of his flannel shirt.

Cody gently brushed her fingers over the spots on the colt's soft, fuzzy forehead. "Stardust," she said.

And so it was that Stardust and Cody began their friendship. And what a great friendship it was! Cody devoted all of her time to the colt and he quickly became attached to her.

All summer long they went for long walks in the bright Montana sun, with the vast Rocky Mountain peaks rising in the distance. When Stardust was near Cody, he followed right behind her like a puppy. When he was out of sight, Cody would only need to blow on her homemade wooden whistle and Stardust would come running as fast as his legs could carry him.

Stardust ate well and grew remarkably fast that summer. Cody always had a pocket full of treats for him—pieces of carrots or slices of fresh apples that Stardust loved. Dad accused Cody of spoiling Stardust, but Cody insisted that she only rewarded him for obeying the shrill tweet of her whistle.

When fall came, Cody went back to school. Although she liked seeing her friends again, she hated leaving Stardust—the schoolhouse was many miles away, and the hours of school and travel left almost no time to spend with him.

Sometimes, after school, she would saddle up Ruby and head out across the ranch with Stardust running alongside. His legs were now less spindly, and he could keep up with his mother. It was great fun!

All too soon Cody could feel a chilly nip in the air. Flocks of geese in V-shaped formations flew south overhead and white peaks of freshly fallen snow now capped the distant mountains.

"Where will Stardust stay this winter?" Cody asked one day as she and Dad were working in the barn.

"In the corral with the other horses," Dad said matter-of-factly.

"But it'll be too cold for him," Cody said. "I've heard winter's going to be very hard this year. Don't you think we could make a stall for him in the barn?"

"No," Dad insisted. "Stardust will be fine. He's already growing his winter coat, and I just fixed the roof on the lean-to. He'll be able to get out of the weather if it gets too bad."

Cody worried about this for several days but her worrying did no good. Stardust was placed in the corral with the herd. So every night, just before bedtime, Cody went out to the corral to say good night. Although he looked tiny in the corral with all of the other horses, Stardust seemed happy.

When the big snows began to fall from the mountains, Cody visited the corral more and more often. Sometimes she would even get out of her bed in the middle of the night, light the lantern, and go out to check on Stardust.

But the big storm of December seventeenth was more than just snow. The wind blew furiously, rattling the shingles and banging the shutters. The drifting snow was mixed with ice and it beat against Cody's bedroom window with a relentless pecking sound. Cody couldn't sleep. Thinking about Stardust, she tossed in bed with every howl the wind made.

Suddenly, Cody heard a loud crash from the direction of the corral. Dressing quickly, Cody put on layers of warm clothing. She wrapped her woolen scarf around her neck and took her oil lamp outside.

Her worst fear became a reality when Cody discovered that a huge branch from the big oak tree had broken off in the storm and fallen on the fence, snapping it like a twig. All of the horses, including Stardust, had panicked and rushed out through the gaping hole in the corral. The tracks in the snow showed that the horses were headed south toward the canyon.

Cody rushed to the bunkhouse to get help. Throwing open the bunkhouse door, she found all of the ranch hands comfortably seated around the glowing potbelly stove.

"Cody!" Andy exclaimed. "What in the world are you doing out on a night like this?"

"Didn't you hear that crash? The corral fence is busted and all of the horses are headed for the canyon," Cody said breathlessly. "We've got to find them and bring them back. Without food or shelter, some of them might not make it through the night."

The ranch hands looked at one another uneasily for several long moments as the wind howled outside and pelted the bunkhouse with icy bits. Finally Nick, the oldest of the ranch hands, reached into the pocket of his vest and casually took out his pipe.

"I don't know about you boys," he said. "But I wouldn't go out in this storm for a month's salary. Besides," he added uncertainly while avoiding Cody's eyes, "I'm sure the horses will be all right."

"Nick's right about one thing, Cody," Andy agreed. "We're staying here in the bunkhouse until the storm blows over. Now you'd better get back to bed."

Reluctantly, Cody left the bunkhouse and started back for her own room. But as she crossed the tracks through the drifting snow, she knew she couldn't wait until morning.

Wrapping her scarf an extra time around her neck and checking the oil in her lamp, Cody set out through the storm in search of Stardust. At first the tracks were easy to follow and walking in the trodden-down snow was no problem. But as Cody went further and further, the snow became deeper and the tracks became obscured by snow drifts.

Although Cody guessed that the horses were heading for the canyon, she had no idea where in the canyon they would be or how she could find them in the storm. The tracks in the snow were now all but gone as she tirelessly trudged along.

Suddenly an idea came to her. She reached into her pocket and found the homemade wooden whistle that Stardust knew so well. Without stopping, Cody put the whistle to her lips and blew hard.

Tweeeeeet! The sound rang out on the waves of the north wind that was blowing right toward the canyon. Cody continued to blow again and again into the night.

Finally, she stopped blowing and looked carefully for any sign of the lost horses. Through the storm a shape appeared. It was Stardust, all alone and covered with a blanket of icy, fresh snowflakes. Cody reached into her pocket again and found a leftover carrot nub. Brushing the snow off her colt's neck, she fed him the treat and gave him a warm hug at the same time.

"Let's go home, boy," Cody said with a feeling of great relief.

As Cody lifted her lamp and turned to start back toward the ranch, she saw another dark shape. It was Ruby, following her colt through the storm. And behind Ruby came the whole herd, all traveling in line, each one following the one in front of it.

A strange procession headed for the corral that night—Cody and her lantern in front, with Stardust, Ruby, and thirty-six other horses behind, all making their way single file through the storm to the shelter of home.

By the time they reached the two big pine trees that marked the edge of the lane, Cody was growing tired from her long journey and was half-frozen as the strong wind blew snow directly at her face. Only the joy of bringing Stardust home kept her going step after step.

Through the darkness up ahead, Cody thought she could see lights moving about. Squinting hard, she realized there *were* lights—coming from a dozen lanterns near the bunkhouse. Dad and Mom had aroused the ranch hands and were preparing a search party. Suddenly the lights moved in one cluster toward Cody and her line of horses.

"Cody!" Dad yelled as he and Mom ran to meet her.

They hugged joyfully. Then Dad saw the line of horses, and a look of disbelief came upon his face.

"How did you do that?" he asked.

"I guess they were all as anxious to get home as Stardust was," Cody explained.

As she walked the horses up the lane to the corral, Cody put her hand in her pocket and clutched the homemade whistle that had helped her save the horses. "It may not look like much," she thought, "but looks aren't everything."

# Adrianna's Chickens

## AN ORIGINAL STORY BY ANNE SCHRAFF

**Spanish Words:**

*Jorge* (pronounced "HOR-hay"): is a Spanish form of George.

*Gracias* (pronounced "GRA-si-as"): means "thank you."

*Pueblo* (pronounced "PWE-blo"): means "town."

*Pollo* (pronounced "PO-yo"): means "chicken."

*Arroz con pollo* (pronounced "arr-ROS kon PO-yo"): means "rice with chicken."

*Pollo frito* (pronounced "PO-yo FREE-to"): means "fried chicken."

Jorge was a poor farmer who lived in Sinaloa, Mexico. After his hard-working wife died, Jorge and his three children struggled to make a living. One day Jorge gathered his children around him and said, "We only have a little money left. We need to invest it wisely. Go to the *pueblo* and choose something that will make life easier for us."

Jorge gave some coins to his oldest son, Carlos, and said, "You are my eldest son and you are wise."

"*Gracias*, Papa," Carlos said with a proud smile.

Jorge gave some coins to his second son, Roberto, and said, "You are younger, but you are also clever." "*Gracias*, Papa," said Roberto.

"What about me?" cried Adrianna, Jorge's only daughter. "Don't I also get some coins?"

Jorge smiled at Adrianna. "You are very sensible, my daughter, but what do you know about spending money wisely?"

"I work side by side with my brothers on the farm," insisted Adrianna, "and I shall make a good choice!"

So Jorge gave Adrianna a few coins too.

"How foolish," grumbled Roberto.

"How silly," snapped Carlos.

Carlos was the oldest and he had the longest legs, so he sprinted ahead of the others. When he reached the town market, Carlos saw vendors selling fruits and vegetables and also animals.

"We have no horse," Carlos thought. "It would be fine indeed to have a horse. He could pull our wagon and Roberto and I could ride him."

Carlos didn't have enough coins to buy a really fine horse. The best work horses were too expensive. So Carlos had to choose between a very old horse or a wild horse. He decided on an untamed, beautiful, black-and-white horse. "I shall gentle him," Carlos said to himself, tying a rope on the horse to lead him home.

When Roberto got to the market with his coins, he looked at sheep and pigs. He had enough coins to buy a large pig. "Mmmm," said Roberto, smacking his lips. "This pig shall grow even fatter when we feed him. Then we will dine on pork and ham!" So Roberto bought the pig, tied a rope around his neck, and led him home.

When Adrianna got to the market, she counted her coins. Her father had given her the fewest coins. One vendor was selling beautiful blue and yellow parrots. Although Adrianna admired the parrots, she knew that would not be a wise purchase. Instead, Adrianna bought two hens and a rooster in a cage. Then she headed home with the cage.

When Carlos and Roberto saw the two hens and the rooster, they laughed so hard they fell on the ground. "Silly little sister," Carlos shouted, slapping his thighs. "Look at those scrawny birds! They aren't enough to make a decent dinner for us!"

"Quit teasing your sister," Jorge said. "She is just a little girl. She does not understand about buying animals."

Adrianna just smiled and built a wire coop for the birds. And then she watched Carlos train his new horse. When Carlos climbed on the horse's back, the horse bucked, threw Carlos into the dirt, and began to run. The wild horse leapt right over the corral fence and ran towards the mountains.

Carlos and Roberto ran after the horse, but the chase was useless. The horse was gone in a cloud of dust.

Roberto grinned and said, "You made a big mistake, Carlos. Only I made a good decision. Soon my pig will be big enough to eat. And what fine meals we will have!"

Adrianna fed her two hens and her rooster and paid no attention to her brothers. Soon, the hens began to lay glossy white eggs. Adrianna gathered some of them and her family had fried eggs and scrambled eggs and omelets.

At last Roberto's pig was big enough to eat. Jorge and his three children dined on pork and ham for many days. But then it was all gone.

By now, fluffy little yellow baby chicks followed Adrianna's two hens around the barnyard. Adrianna had not taken *all* the eggs. The hens sat on some and hatched big broods of baby chicks.

"Ahhh," Jorge cried, "we will have many chicken dinners on Sunday—*arroz con pollo, pollo frito!*"

Adrianna smiled quietly and built a bigger chicken coop. Soon the baby chicks grew up and they were laying eggs. So Adrianna took baskets of eggs to the market and sold them. After a while, they had so many roosters that even though Jorge and his family had chicken every Sunday, they had enough roosters to sell.

"We have never had such a good life," cried Jorge, "and it is all because of Adrianna's chickens!"

But Adrianna had little to say. She had an even bigger idea. She had cooked so many chicken dinners for her family that she was now an expert. Everybody said Adrianna's chicken dishes were the best in Sinaloa.

So Adrianna put Carlos and Roberto to work

building a restaurant in front of their house. It was right on the highway and soon many people were coming to taste Adrianna's *pollo.*

Adrianna wore a big white chef's hat and her long, glossy black hair was tied in braids. She had to hire someone to help her cook and wash dishes, so she hired Carlos and Roberto. Her restaurant made so much money that Carlos and Roberto could afford to buy a fine horse and many pigs. And even though her brothers had laughed at Adrianna when she brought home those first three skinny birds, Adrianna didn't ever say "I told you so," except maybe once or twice.

# Liza and the Lost Letter

AN ORIGINAL STORY BY BRUCE LANSKY

If you ever go to London to attend a festive royal event, a wedding perhaps, you'll have to wade through throngs of cheering, waving people to catch a glimpse of royalty.

But it's not like that when the royal family is staying in Balmoral Castle, their summer palace nestled in the rolling green hills of the Scottish countryside. There, you often see them riding through town in a horse-drawn carriage, surrounded by a small guard clad in bright red and black.

Every Sunday morning at nine o'clock, the royal

family rides past Liza Higgins' house, and Liza is always waiting on the sidewalk in front of her house, waving a little British flag—a one-girl welcoming committee. The first time Liza ever saw the royal carriage, Princess Margaret waved at her. Since then, Liza had come out to watch the royal family ride by every summer Sunday, rain or shine.

One Sunday morning in June, as the royal carriage rolled towards her, Liza noticed that Princess Margaret was reading a letter. Suddenly, the letter flew out of the princess' hand into the air. The carriage jerked to a stop. The guards dismounted and began searching the street.

Liza watched the wind blow the letter into a small alley. She noticed how anxious the princess looked. But the queen seemed impatient. She spoke to the driver, and just as suddenly as the procession had stopped, the guards mounted and the carriage resumed moving down the street.

Liza waited until the carriage and guards were out of sight. Curious, she walked down the cobblestone street to where she had seen the carriage stop. No one else was out on the street yet—most people were still eating breakfast or dressing for church. Liza walked up the alley where she had seen the letter blow.

There, behind a trash barrel, was a handwritten letter on fine stationery imprinted with the seal of the king of France. As she glanced briefly at the letter, Liza noticed that it was written in French. Liza folded the letter carefully and put it in her pocket. She tried to stay calm as she strolled back to her house.

Liza didn't tell a soul about what she had found. All through breakfast she wondered what to do. If she were the princess, she would want the letter back, unread, and the entire matter kept in the strictest confidence. At church that day, a sermon on the golden rule strengthened Liza's resolve to return the letter as soon as possible.

Once the service was over, Liza told her parents that she wanted to take a walk and set off at a brisk pace for the summer palace, which was about a mile from church.

The gate to the palace was guarded by a gatekeeper who was wearing a tall, bushy, black hat and standing still as a statue.

"Excuse me," said Liza, "but I must see Princess Margaret."

"May I see your pass?" inquired the guard brusquely.

"I don't have a pass," answered Liza.

"I'm sorry. No one can get through the gate without a pass," responded the guard without moving a single body part other than his jaw.

"But you don't understand," insisted Liza. "I've found something that belongs to the princess. I'm sure she'll want it back."

"And, no doubt, you'll be wanting a reward for your service."

"No, I just want to return to the princess what is hers."

"In that case, come back when you have a pass," he said, avoiding her glance.

"But how will I ever get a pass?" asked Liza, who was growing frustrated by the delay.

"I'll be happy to arrange it—for just half the reward," he answered.

Puzzled, Liza asked, "Are you serious?"

Without even looking at Liza, the gatekeeper simply said, "Good day."

Liza didn't move. She was angered by the gatekeeper's greed, but the thought of a reward hadn't even occurred to her. So she reconsidered and said, "Perhaps I will give you half the reward."

For the first time the gatekeeper smiled. He took a piece of paper out of his pocket and signed it. "Here," he said as he opened the gate for Liza and let her in. "Now remember—this pass will cost you half the reward."

"How can I ever forget your kindness?" Liza responded sarcastically.

Another guard escorted Liza to the foyer, where the appointments secretary, who was seated at an ornate wooden desk, was idly turning the pages of a huge appointment book.

"Who is this urchin?" the secretary called out scornfully to the guard.

"Just another beggar looking for a royal reward," answered the guard. "She claims she is returning something to the princess."

"I'm sorry, but Her Majesty's calendar is completely full—for weeks. She has no time to meet with you. But, if you'll just give whatever it is to me, I'll see that it is returned to the princess."

Liza shook her head. "You don't understand, this is a personal matter. I must return it to the princess myself."

"In that case, come back in September and I'll see

what I can do. Good day."

"That's ridiculous!" protested Liza. "The royal family will have moved back to Buckingham Palace by then."

Liza did not move. She stared into the eyes of the appointments secretary, so he would know she was serious. "Why don't you ask Princess Margaret if she's lost something. I think you'll find that she will want to see me immediately."

The secretary looked down at his book again. "I'll see. If it's that important, then perhaps I can accommodate you. But you'll have to compensate me for my efforts on your behalf. It will cost you half of your reward."

Liza was quickly learning the ways of the royal court. She spoke through clenched teeth as she controlled her temper, "Agreed." Then she sat down to wait.

In less than five minutes the appointments secretary returned. "You're in luck," he smiled. "The princess will see you. Remember—I get half the reward."

"I have an excellent memory," Liza assured him.

The secretary ushered Liza into Princess Margaret's chamber. As they entered, the princess was pacing the floor. On her face was the same worried expression that Liza had observed when the letter had blown out of her hands.

When Liza entered, the princess paused in her pacing. "Thank you," she said to the appointments secretary. "That will be all." He left, closing the polished mahogany door behind him.

"And who might you be?" Princess Margaret inquired.

"Liza Higgins, Your Majesty," Liza answered as she curtsied politely.

"I am curious to know, what have you found?" the princess asked Liza anxiously

"A letter, Your Majesty. I believe you lost it on the way to church this morning." Liza retrieved the letter from her jacket pocket as the princess approached her.

Taking the letter that Liza held out for her, the princess opened it. A huge smile covered her face. "Thank God!" she exclaimed. Then she looked at Liza. "Have you read it?"

"No," said Liza. The princess peered into Liza's eyes to see if she was telling the truth. "You see," Liza continued, "I can't understand a word of French." The princess smiled.

"Have you shown it to anyone?" the princess inquired.

"Not a soul, Your Majesty."

The princess breathed a sigh of relief. "Thank you, Liza. This letter means a great deal to me. Is there anything I can do for you? Name your reward."

Liza took a moment to think before answering. "I did not return your letter for a reward. I was just doing for you what I would have liked someone to do for me. But since you are so kind as to offer a reward, I cannot refuse." She paused, still working out the details of her request.

"However, before I make my request, I wonder if you would summon the palace gatekeeper and your appointments secretary. They both helped me to gain an audience with you. I think they will be happy to know that you have granted me a reward."

"Certainly," said the princess. "Guard!"

Instantly, the door opened and a guard appeared. Princess Margaret summoned the gatekeeper and her secretary. When they had arrived, she repeated her offer, "Liza, you have done a great service to me by returning a prized possession. How can I reward you? Your wish is my command."

The gatekeeper and the secretary smiled with anticipation.

"Thank you for your generosity, Your Majesty," Liza began. "If you will grant my wish, I humbly request a sentence of two weeks in jail."

The faces of the gatekeeper and the secretary turned white. Their jaws dropped open.

The princess frowned. "I don't understand..."

"You see, although I did not seek a reward, the royal gatekeeper made me promise to give him half of my reward in return for letting me in through the palace gate. And your appointments secretary made me promise to give him half of my reward in return for letting me see you today—even though I told them both that I was here to return something you had lost.

"I hope that you will grant my request, giving half of my reward to the gatekeeper and half to your secretary to fulfill my promise."

"I cannot refuse your request," the princess said, smiling broadly. "Guards, take the prisoners away."

Then, turning to Liza, she said, "Young lady, you have done two great services: one to me personally, and one to the royal family. I have divided the reward for your first service as you requested. But as a reward for your second service—ridding the palace of greed—I would like to give you another reward."

As the princess took a close look at Liza, she said, "You look vaguely familiar. Are you the girl who waves to me every Sunday morning as we drive to church?"

"Yes, Your Majesty. I wait for you every Sunday. Once you even waved to me."

"Well," answered Princess Margaret, "Next Sunday, instead of watching me drive by, how would you like to join me for a ride in the royal carriage—dressed in a brand-new gown?"

"I'd love to!" gasped Liza.

If you had been on Drury Lane that next Sunday morning at nine o'clock, you would have seen Liza, dressed in a beautiful lavender satin gown given to her by Princess Margaret, sitting next to the princess in the royal carriage, waving happily to a huge crowd of friends and family members who had, for the first time anyone can remember, gotten up early on a Sunday morning to cheer Liza and the royal family as they drove by on the way to church.

# Jamila and the Lion

## AN ORIGINAL STORY BY ANNE SCHRAFF

**African Musical Instruments:**
*Mbira* (pronounced "mBEE-ra"): a musical instrument similar
  to a small piano.
*Maraca* (pronounced "ma-RA-ka"): a type of rattle.

Long ago a little girl named Jamila lived in Luhula,
a small African village east of Nigeria on the Ubangi
River. She grew up in a thatched-roof hut with her
parents and her two brothers. Jamila's father, Ahmed,
was the leader of the village. He settled the villagers'
disputes, solved problems, and presided over ceremonies.

One year Luhula faced a very big problem—a huge lion was terrorizing the village. Luhula was at the edge of the great savanna where lions hunted for antelope. But this lion preferred to prey on the farm animals raised by the villagers.

As they always did in times of trouble, the villagers turned to Ahmed for guidance. A large crowd gathered outside his hut and the people were all talking at once.

"Ahmed," cried one farmer, "the terrible lion has carried away two of my goats."

"The terrible lion has carried away three of my pigs," groaned another farmer.

"I know," said Ahmed. "The terrible lion has eaten most of my chickens! And worst of all, I fear for the people of Luhula. What if the lion carries off our women and children?"

"I would swat the beast with a broom," said Laini, Ahmed's wife.

Jamila, who was standing next to her mother, laughed. Ahmed looked very sternly at his wife and daughter. "Do not make a joke of this. You are not hunters like the men. You have not faced the lion's jaws!"

"Tell us what to do, Ahmed," the villagers pleaded.

"I shall lead the men of Luhula on a great hunt. We

shall carry our sharpest spears. My own sons, Jelani and Saliim, are the bravest hunters in Luhula. With their help we will slay the lion," Ahmed announced to the cheering crowd.

Before Ahmed left on the hunt with his sons, he gave strict orders for his wife and daughter to remain inside their hut.

"But I must bake bread in the outdoor oven," Laini said.

"And I must fetch water from the river," said Jamila who loved to hear the water gurgle in the jug.

"You must both remain inside," Ahmed said. "The lion may come back to the village." And off the men went on the great hunt.

Days passed and Jamila was getting tired of staying inside the house. "The hunters have been gone a long time. We are running low on water," she said. "When will they return?"

"I hope the lion didn't eat them all," Laini worried. "Our men are not as great at hunting as they think they are. When they sing their boastful hunting songs, their heads swell with foolish pride!"

Jamila remembered the celebration after the last hunt; the villagers accompanied the men's songs with music—the tinkle of mbiras, the rattle of maracas, the blare of horns, and the thunder of drums rocked the village. She also remembered that the lion did not bother the villagers that day. Could the lion have been scared of the loud sounds?

"Look, Mother," gasped Jamila as she peered from the window. "It's the lion!"

Right through the middle of the village walked a huge lion. He did not seem to be in any hurry as he strolled lazily to the chicken coop.

"I wish I had a spear," Laini cried, "but the men took them all!"

"I am so angry that the lion has taken over our village," Jamila said. "He eats our animals while we cower in our houses like timid little rabbits!"

When the lion had eaten a few chickens, he walked from the village on the narrow trail that led into the jungle.

Soon after that, Ahmed and the men returned from the great hunt. "We failed," Ahmed groaned. "The moment that giant beast heard the swish of our spears through the air, he vanished like smoke in the brush."

"We cannot find him," complained Jelani, the

elder brother.

"So we cannot slay him," said Saliim, the younger brother.

"What can we do?" demanded the terrified villagers.

"I have the answer," said Jelani. "The terrible lion always comes by the narrow trail. We must barricade it with branches."

"Fool," said Saliim, "lions climb over branches."

"Silence," demanded Ahmed. "We must face the truth. The lion cannot be slain. He cannot be driven away. We must leave Luhula and find another place to live."

"Why are we letting the lion drive us from our own homes and farmlands?" cried Jamila. "Are we not smarter than the lion?"

Jelani sneered, "Listen to the brave little bird! What does she know of lions?"

"Yes," snickered Saliim, "how the little girl does flap her lips. Tell us, Jamila, will you take a spear and slay the terrible lion?"

But Jamila was no longer listening to her brothers. She remembered the hunting songs and the loud music again. She trembled with excitement as an idea took shape in her mind.

Jamila walked from house to house in the village. She told the women and girls of her idea and their eyes glowed with excitement and hope.

That night, as large clouds covered the moon, Jamila and the girls and women of the village crept from their houses, carrying drums, panpipes, mbiras, bells, maracas, and horns. And when the moon was full, the lion moved down his favorite path on his way to finish off the chickens, goats, and pigs of the village.

Suddenly, as the lion appeared, the quiet night was shattered with the piercing blasts of panpipes, the booming clang of bells, and the loud rattle of maracas. Mbiras tinkled and the great horns howled fiercely. Small girls blew whistles and Jamila pounded on a big drum.

The lion reared back, his eyes wild with terror. The sounds attacked his tender eardrums and shocked his brain. The lion clawed the air in desperation, but the sounds grew louder and more deafening. And then, scared to his very bones, the lion turned tail and ran as fast as he could. He didn't stop running until he was swallowed up in the tall savanna grass, far from Luhula. It was doubtful he would ever want to find his way back to the village. But if he did, Jamila knew how to drive him away.

The hunters, drawn by the thunder of music in the night, stood open-mouthed and awe-struck. Jamila, still holding her drum, turned, smiled, and explained, "Lions do not like your sharp spears. And, apparently, they do not like loud noises either."

Jelani looked down at the dirt. Saliim fiddled with the long chain around his neck. Laini smiled proudly while Ahmed came to his daughter and placed his hands upon her shoulders. "From now on," he announced with a proud smile, "you are Jamila, defender of the village."

# The Peacemakers

### An Original Story by Lois Greiman

"We've come too far, Flint," Jessie said, putting a hand on her mare's dappled neck.

The doe they'd been racing was gone and the woods here were thick and silent. Mists curled up from the earth, seeming to reach for them with cool, ghostlike arms.

Darkness would set in soon and she was on MacDuff land. The thought sent a tingle of fear spurting up her spine.

"Father would kill me if he knew where we are," Jessie whispered. Flint tossed her head in agreement. "Take me home, girl," Jessie said, reining the mare away. But, suddenly, she heard a noise behind her.

Jessie turned and gasped. A horse stepped through the mist. He was large and black and upon his back was a girl about twelve years of age, no older than Jessie herself.

They stared at each other in surprise for a moment, but then the other girl spoke.

"Do you hate me?" she asked quietly.

"Hate you?" Jessie whispered. Who was this girl who had appeared out of nowhere? "How could I hate you? I don't even know you."

"But you're an Armstrong. I can tell by the plaid beneath your saddle." She pointed to Jessie's blue saddle blanket, then to the green cloth beneath her own. "And I am a MacDuff."

Jessie caught her breath. Her father had warned her about their enemies. They were thieves, and worse, not to be trusted—not like the Armstrongs who were honorable Scots. But when Jessie stared at the girl in front of her, she could see very little difference between them. The girl's light brown hair hung down her back in a long fat braid just as Jessie's did. Wisps of it had escaped as if she, too, had just had a wild ride through the heather.

"What's your name?" Jessie asked softly.

"Marnie," answered the other. "I rode out with the hunters, but I could not bear to see the deer slain, so I left them to ride on my own."

Jessie nodded. "I, too, hate to see deer die. In fact, I followed one here, for she was so beautiful to watch. But my father, the lord of the Armstrongs, will be angry if he learns how far I have come. He says my little brother, Douglas, and I will turn his hair gray, for we are always exploring in the forest outside the castle walls and pretending we are great heroes."

Marnie smiled. "We are not so different, you and I," she said. "For my father, the lord of the MacDuffs, would be quite upset if he knew I was out so late. I, too, have a brother, though I don't think he's ever done anything so awful as to speak to a horrible Armstrong."

Jessie thought that perhaps she should be insulted, but Marnie laughed and Jessie could not help smiling. "I don't think I'm horrible. And I don't think you're so horrible either—for a MacDuff."

Marnie laughed again. "Perhaps we could be friends. Perhaps no one would have to know. We could meet here next week and learn more about each other."

Jessie was about to answer, but suddenly she heard

a noise behind her. "Father has probably sent men out to find me. I must go. But I will meet you here a week from tonight."

"Yes," said Marnie. "In one week."

The two parted, but a week later they met again. Leaving their horses to graze in the woods, they walked amid the trees and talked.

"Whatever started this foolish feud between our families in the first place?" Jessie asked.

Marnie shrugged. "I don't think anyone even remembers for certain."

"Then it is time to end it," Jessie said.

"I wish we could. Oh look," said Marnie, "black currants. If my mother were here she would boil the currant leaves and make an ointment that's good for cuts and wounds. She's a great healer, you know."

Jessie scowled. "My mother died five years ago, right after Douglas was born. But..." she said, and smiled, "if my aunt Agnes were here she would pick the currants and bake some tarts."

"And my father would eat them," Marnie said with a laugh. "There's nothing he likes better than sweets, and my mother never bakes tarts." She stopped and turned toward her new friend. "It seems there is much our families could learn from each other."

"Yes," said Jessie. "So let's learn."

From then on, the girls secretly met every week. And each week their friendship grew. Meanwhile, the feud between their families continued, stronger than ever.

One night a band of MacDuff men crept onto Armstrong land and stole some sheep.

A few nights later the Armstrongs stole ten head of fat cattle from the MacDuffs.

The MacDuffs, in turn, raided the Armstrong's herds. That night Jessie's little brother, Douglas, was out exploring the hills in the moonlight. He was not with his big sister this time, since he wanted to prove to Jessie that he was a brave warrior. So when he saw the raiders, he crept through the ferns until he was very near one man. Then he drew his wooden sword and jumped up. The man he attacked was surprised by the small figure that seemed to appear out of nowhere. He swung wildly with his sword and nicked the boy's arm.

Douglas gasped in pain. His arm burned like fire. He stumbled backward. The man with the sword followed slowly. "I'm sorry. I didn't realize you were just a lad," he said, but Douglas was terrified now. Spinning around, he raced toward home and his father.

"They will pay!" yelled Lord Armstrong.

Jessie awoke because of the noise and hurried down the wooden stairs. Douglas was huddled up near the fire in the great hall where they ate. But above the blanket that was wrapped about him, she could see that his arm was bandaged.

"What happened?" she whispered.

"It was the MacDuffs!" her father raged. "They have raided our herds again. But this time they have wounded my son too. And now they will pay!"

"What will you do?" she asked.

"I will hurt someone that is as dear to Lord MacDuff as my son is to me," he said.

"But..." Jessie managed to take a step closer. She loved her father, and she knew he loved her, but when he was angry, it frightened her. "Perhaps they did not mean to hurt Douglas. Perhaps it was a mistake."

"Yes, it certainly *was* a mistake," Jessie's father thundered. "A mistake MacDuff will sorely regret when his own son is wounded."

Jessie gasped. Her father meant to hurt Marnie's brother. Then the MacDuffs would wound an Armstrong. And then, perhaps, the Armstrongs would kill a MacDuff.

"No, Father, please," she pleaded. "Don't do this. There must be another way to settle this."

Her father stared at her and in his eyes she saw his sadness. "This is the way it must be," he said. "I will have an eye for an eye and a tooth for a tooth. Everything they do to us, we will do to them."

Jessie held her breath. "Everything?" she asked.

"Yes," vowed her father. "Everything they do to the Armstrongs we will do to the MacDuffs, and more."

That afternoon Jessie was supposed to meet Marnie, but her father ordered her to stay in the castle. Jessie wanted to obey him, but she knew the only way to prevent more trouble was to speak to her friend. So she sneaked out when no one was looking.

A few minutes later, she was racing Flint bareback through the woods. Branches grabbed at her. They scratched her hands until the wounds bled, but she knew what she had to do.

"Marnie!" Jessie gasped. She pulled Flint to a halt. "I'm so glad you came."

Marnie looked pale and worried. "I listened while the men were talking. I know a boy was hurt and I am sorry."

"Douglas' arm is badly cut." Jessie wiped the blood

from the back of her hand onto the skirt of her gown. She had no time to worry about herself now.

"It was your brother who was wounded?" Marnie asked.

"Yes. He crept from his room to go exploring in the hills. It's all my fault—I was the one who taught him how to sneak from the castle without anyone knowing. And now he's hurt because of it."

Marnie shook her head. "It's not your fault, Jessie. Oh! I hate this ridiculous feud. If our families were friends, my mother could heal Douglas' arm."

"That's just what I came to talk to you about," Jessie said. "If we don't do something to stop this feud, someone else will be hurt. Maybe it will be a MacDuff. Maybe it will even be your brother. My father has vowed to get revenge."

"But what can we do?" asked Marnie. "We're not the lords of our clans."

"No, we're not lords," Jessie said. "But we're smart enough to know this feud must end. And I know how we can end it."

Jessie didn't sleep well that night. Nightmares haunted her. But when she walked to the drawbridge the next morning, she made herself act as if nothing were different.

"Good morning, Malcom," she said to the watch-man. "Will you let me out so I can—" She stopped talking as she gazed out at the bridge. A large jar stood there. She knew, then, that Marnie had convinced her mother to help with their plan. But she pretended to know nothing. "What is that sitting on the bridge?"

"Why, it looks like a jug of some sort," Malcom said in surprise.

"Let's see what it is," suggested Jessie.

In a minute Malcom held the jar in his hands. Lifting the cloth that covered it, he peered inside. "I don't know what it is," he said, "but it smells of herbs."

"There's a note," said Jessie, lifting up the piece of leather with writing on it.

"What does it say?"

Jessie was proud of the fact that she could read. Many people in her clan couldn't. "It says, 'This is an ointment to heal the lad's arm. Put it on the wound twice a day.' And it is signed, 'MacDuff.'"

Malcom raised his brows in surprise. "You'd best take that to our lord right away," he said.

When Jessie found her father, he scowled down at the note she handed him. He read it aloud, then read it again. "What kind of trick is this?" he asked.

"Maybe it's not a trick," Jessie said. "Maybe the MacDuffs just want to help."

"The MacDuffs never want to help," he said. "This stuff will probably only make Douglas' arm worse. The herbs in it could be poison. I'm throwing it out."

"No," Jessie pleaded. "Please. Look, I have a scratch on my hand. Let me put some of the ointment on that. If it doesn't get worse, we can try it on Douglas' wound."

Jessie's father reluctantly agreed. She smeared the fragrant stuff onto her hand. By evening her scratch looked better.

That night they covered Douglas' wound in the ointment and wrapped it in a bandage. By morning his arm didn't hurt as much and the swelling had gone down.

Jessie looked up from Douglas' arm and into her father's eyes. "Well," she said, trying to be brave, "I guess it's time you fulfilled your vow."

"What vow?" Lord Armstrong demanded.

"You said that whatever the MacDuffs do, you will do back plus more."

"What are you talking about, lass? I meant that I

would make them pay for their crimes."

"You vowed that you would do the same thing they did," she reminded him.

"But..." Her father paced across the great hall. "That's nonsense. We don't even know how to make this healing ointment."

"Then give them something else," Jessie said. "Something nice."

Her father stared at her for a second. "Don't be foolish," he said.

"So your promises mean nothing?" Jessie asked.

"Of course I keep my promises," he said, looking angry.

"Then give them something good," Jessie pleaded.

That night, Lord Armstrong himself sneaked across MacDuff land. But this time he hadn't come to steal. Instead, he left a basket not far from the castle wall. In it was a bolt of fine velvet cloth and a note that read, "This is for the MacDuffs, from the Armstrongs."

Jessie was too nervous to sleep that night or the night after that. But when she hurried down to the gate a day later, she found a basket on the bridge. The basket was lined with the green cloth of the MacDuff clan and was filled with plump black currants. She took them to the kitchen where Aunt Agnes made them into sweet, crusty tarts.

That night Lord Armstrong took the tarts to the MacDuffs, but when he bent to set them on the bridge, the lord of the MacDuffs stepped out of hiding.

The two men stared at each other.

"I have heard that your son was wounded," said Lord MacDuff, "and I am sorry. But I am glad that we have been tricked into ending this feud."

"Tricked?" asked Lord Armstrong. "How do you mean?"

"I've discovered that our daughters have been meeting in the woods. It seems they have become friends."

"Jessie knows that is forbidden," Lord Armstrong said. "She would never sneak out to—" But then he stopped to listen. From the darkness, they could hear whispers. "Who's out there?" he called.

Jessie and Marnie stepped from their hiding place. They had followed their fathers there.

Lord Armstrong's mouth fell open. "Jessie!" he said in surprise. "My daughter *would* sneak out, it seems."

"Yes, Father," she said quietly. "I would do almost anything to end the feud between the Armstrongs and the MacDuffs."

For a moment her father didn't speak, but then he nodded. Walking forward, he offered Lord MacDuff his hand in friendship. "It seems our daughters are wiser than we. For them we must end this feud."

"Yes, we will end it for them," said Lord MacDuff. Then he sniffed. Lord Armstrong was still holding the basket of the sweet currant tarts and the delicious smell was strong in the night air. "We will become friends for the sake of our children and for a taste of the sweet-smelling pastry in your basket. Come, we will eat the sweets together while our daughters decide what other ideas they have for the future."

"As a matter of fact," Jessie said as she winked at Marnie, "we've thought of several things already."

# Kim's Surprise Witness

ADAPTED BY BRUCE LANSKY
FROM A CHINESE FOLKTALE

**Vietnamese Word:**

*Dong* (pronounced "dong"): Vietnamese money. In Vietnam, people use dongs instead of dollars.

When Duc Tung, the moneylender, paid a visit, he always brought bad news with him. His scowling face and dark, formal clothes reminded people that if they failed to repay a loan that was due, the consequences would be serious. He would not hesitate to evict a family from their home if they missed a payment. His reputation for ruthlessness had spread throughout the Hanoi province in Vietnam.

Kim was pulling weeds from a rice paddy when Duc Tung arrived in a small carriage driven by two oxen. He stopped the carriage, climbed out, and cleared his throat to get her attention.

"I need to see your parents, young lady. Where are they?" he demanded in a brusque tone of voice.

Kim knew better than to give Duc Tung any information. Her parents would not want him following them around demanding money.

"My parents are very busy. You'll have to come back some other time," Kim explained politely.

"I must see them today," insisted Duc Tung, looking annoyed. "It is a matter of great importance. If you know where they are, I demand that you tell me."

Kim knew exactly where her parents were, but because she did not want Duc Tung to find them, she spoke in riddles: "Because you insist, I will tell you. My father has gone to cut living trees to plant dead trees. My mother has gone to sell the sun and buy the moon. And now that I have told you where they are, I bid you good day." Kim bowed slightly and returned to her gardening.

Duc Tung looked puzzled. He scratched his head and cleared his throat again. "Don't joke with me, young lady. This is a very serious matter. I will ask you one more time where your parents are. I expect a serious answer."

"My answer was not meant as a joke. You asked me where my parents were. I answered truthfully. If you cannot solve the riddles, then I suppose you will have to come back some other time."

A sly smile came over Duc Tung's face. "Perhaps you do not want me to know where your parents are because you think that I have come to collect the money they owe me. You are a very loyal daughter. Your parents would be very proud of you. However, I have good news for your parents. I am sure your parents will be very happy to see me."

"I'm sure they would be happy to see you if they did not owe you any money," Kim answered shrewdly.

"How clever of you to guess," said Duc Tung. "Your parents will be happy to see me because I have come to tell your parents that I have canceled their debt. They do not owe me a single dong. Now please tell me where I can find them," he said.

"It is very kind of you to forgive my parents' debt,"

answered Kim. "It is also very unusual. I need a witness."

"But there's no one else here," said Duc Tung as he sat down on a log. Suddenly, he shrieked and jumped off the log.

"What's the matter?" asked Kim.

"I almost sat on top of a snapping turtle that was sitting on the log," he answered.

"It's only a small turtle," said Kim. "Why are you so afraid of it?"

"Well, if you must know," answered Duc Tung as he regained his composure, "a snapper bit off my little toe when I was a child. I've been scared of them ever since."

"In that case, this snapping turtle will be my witness," Kim announced.

"An excellent idea," said Duc Tung solemnly. "I swear on my ancestors' graves with this snapping turtle as a witness that I have forgiven your parents' debt."

"I believe you are telling the truth, so I will tell you where my parents are. My father is working on the riverbank cutting down bamboo trees to build a fence. My mother is at the market, selling paper fans that she makes to buy oil for her lamp. Thank you again for your generosity."

Later that day Kim's father returned home with his

face knotted in anger.

"What's the matter, Father?" Kim asked.

"While I was working on the riverbank, building a fence, Duc Tung showed up demanding to be paid the money I owed him. I had to give him the bamboo stakes I had cut down. That man is like a snapping turtle. Once he has you in his jaws, he never lets go. I have no idea how he found me."

"Father, I am sorry to say that I told him where you were."

"How could you do that? You know how dangerous he is."

"All too well, Father. But he said he had good news for you—that he was forgiving your debt. I'm sorry to say that I believed him."

"You did your best. Now I must do my best to raise five hundred dongs. Tomorrow I must meet him in court with the rest of the money we owe him or we will lose the farm."

Just then Kim's mother came back from the market, looking upset. "That horrible moneylender, Duc Tung, tracked me down at the market. He took the money I had made selling the fans."

"He tricked me into telling him where you were,

Mother. I'm terribly sorry," Kim explained, trying hard not to cry, for she felt that she had let her parents down.

"Don't worry, Kim," said Kim's mother in a comforting voice. "He would have found us eventually."

That evening Kim's parents visited friends and relatives, trying to scrape up the money they owed Duc Tung. And Kim spent the evening on the bank of the rice paddy, trying to remember everything that had happened that day, so she would be ready for her first visit to the court.

When the judge called the court to order the next morning, Kim and her parents were on one side of the room; Duc Tung was on the other, glaring at them.

In a loud voice, the judge asked: "Have you brought the five hundred dongs that you owe Duc Tung in repayment of the money he loaned to buy your farm?"

"Yes, Your Honor," Kim's father answered grimly, for he had gotten no sleep the night before.

"Bring it to me so that I can count it," commanded the judge.

To her parents' amazement, Kim stepped in front of her father. "Your Honor, there is no reason to pay Duc Tung a single dong. He canceled his debt to my parents."

"Is that true, Duc Tung?" asked the judge.

"Your Honor, the child is making this up."

The judge turned back to Kim. "When did he cancel the debt?"

"Yesterday, Your Honor, when he visited our farm. You see, he asked me where my parents were, but I would not tell him. Then he said that he wanted to see them so he could tell them the good news: that he had forgiven their debt. Naturally, I was so happy that I told him where they were. But when he tracked them down, he took all the money they had with them."

"Is that true?" the judge asked Duc Tung.

"It is nonsense, Your Honor. I didn't visit the farm yesterday. I had more important things to do," said Duc Tung scornfully.

"Well, young lady, I hope you have a witness," said the judge sternly. "I have known Duc Tung a long time, but I have never known him to cancel debts that are owed him."

"I knew no one would believe me," answered Kim, "so I made sure I had a witness, Your Honor."

For the first time that day, Kim's parents smiled. The judge's mouth fell open in amazement. "You do? Who is it?" he asked.

"I have brought my witness in this box," Kim stated confidently, holding the box out in front of her.

Duc Tung began to laugh. "Ha ha ha! The poor girl has lost her mind. She has brought her witness in a little wooden box. Excuse me, Your Honor. This is too funny."

Kim's parents squirmed in embarrassment. "Kim, don't be foolish," her father said. "Put away the box. Let me pay the money I owe and be done with it."

"If you have a witness in that box, I would like to see it," said the judge. "Produce your witness."

"I will give Duc Tung the honor of producing the witness," Kim said as she walked over to Duc Tung and handed the wooden box to him.

But Duc Tung refused to take the box. Suddenly, there was panic on his face and he yelled, "Your Honor, tell her to keep that snapping turtle away from me!"

"Ah ha!" exclaimed the judge, his eyebrows almost reaching the top of his forehead. Then, turning to Kim, the judge ordered, "Young lady, don't keep the court in suspense. Show me what is in your box this instant!"

All eyes were on Kim as she removed the top of the wooden box, reached inside, and pulled out the wriggling snapping turtle, which she held in front of Duc

Tung. "Here is my witness."

Duc Tung leaped away. "That's close enough! That snapper almost bit me yesterday."

"It seems that you recognize her witness," said the judge. "It is obvious that you met Kim yesterday and swore that you had forgiven her parents' debt, with the turtle as a witness. I hereby order the five-hundred-dong debt forgiven. Furthermore, I order you to return the money you collected yesterday from Kim's parents," the judge concluded.

Kim let out a whoop of joy. But, as happy as Kim's parents were when they heard the verdict, they wisely refrained from hugging her until she had put her witness back in the wooden box.

# Vassilisa the Wise

ADAPTED BY JOANNE MITCHELL
FROM A RUSSIAN FOLKTALE

Vassilisa looked out of the window and sighed. Would the rain never stop? Her brother, Nickolai, had been gone for days. He went to visit Prince Aleksei at court to pledge his loyalty. Now that Nickolai had come of age, he would be the Prince's vassal, as their father had been before him. Vassilisa had been left at their country estate, with Grandmother, to supervise the peasants as they tended the crops.

Vassilisa imagined Nickolai at the center of a lively, amusing crowd. What a grand time he must be having! What exciting tales he would have to tell when he returned home!

At court Nickolai fretted at the delay. He still had not been able to pay his respects to the Prince, who was much too busy to spare time for an unimportant country lord. The lively, elegant crowd at court made no attempt to hide their scorn for Nickolai's country accent and clothes. Would he never be free to return to his estate?

One day an archery match was held. The crowd cheered as one soldier hit the center of the target and then sent another arrow so close to the first you could not have fit a thread between them.

"You won't see shooting that fine in your little village," an officer remarked to Nickolai. "You have to come to court for that."

"Oh, I don't know," Nickolai said, stung by the officer's tone. "In my village we have many fine archers. Even my sister, Vassilisa, could do better than that."

"Oh, ho!" cried the officer, laughing. "Do you hear that, Ivan? This countryman claims that his sister can outshoot you!"

"I tremble in fear," said Ivan. "When can we hold a match?" The crowd laughed and Nickolai flushed in irritation.

Later that day a horse race was held. At the end of

the race the same officer cried out, "Does your village also excel in horsemanship, countryman?"

"Yes," Nickolai replied, growing angry. "We have many fine horses and many fine riders. Even my sister can outride anyone at court." Everyone laughed and Nickolai gritted his teeth.

At the feast that night in the great hall, Nickolai sat alone. Course after course was brought in on golden platters: spicy haunch of venison, wild boar roasted with berries, pigeons baked with honey. Golden goblets of mead were placed on the table. For all he tasted of these delicacies, Nickolai might as well have been eating gruel and water. Other diners looked at Nickolai, whispered to each other, and smiled.

When the minstrels began to play, one of the courtiers said loudly, "I wonder if his sister also sings and plays better than any at court."

"No, but I can," said Nickolai. "However, I did not bring my lyre with me to court."

A roar of laughter went up from the surrounding people. At the head table, Prince Aleksei turned to look. At his side the lovely Princess Svetlana, his niece, also turned to look. "What is it?" the Prince asked.

"Your highness," one of the courtiers replied, "this

country oaf boasts about his village and his sister. She can outshoot your best archer and outride your best horseman, he claims. And now he claims he himself is a finer musician than any of your minstrels. Alas," the man said with a smirk, "he cannot prove the latter because he did not bring his lyre to court."

"Come here," Prince Aleksei commanded Nickolai. When Nickolai stood before him, he continued, "So it seems you have a remarkable sister. What else does she do? Is she beautiful and clever and wealthy as well? Does she spin hay into threads of gold?"

Nickolai fumed at the mockery in the Prince's voice. "My sister is not wealthy, my Prince. But she is indeed beautiful. She has braids of pale gold, thick as my wrist and long enough to sit on. She is more beautiful than any woman in court." The listening crowd gasped.

Princess Svetlana stiffened. Her dark eyes flashed in anger. "Must I listen to his insults?"

"And she is clever, my sister is," Nickolai continued wildly. "Even more clever than you are, Prince." A hush fell over the room and Nickolai knew he had said too much.

Prince Aleksei stood up. "Guards! To the dungeon with him. Send soldiers to fetch this paragon of sisters to court, so that we may see for ourselves how exceptional she is."

Nickolai's servant, Pyotr, saw his master being taken away by the guards. Slipping away, he rode through the forest by the light of the full moon to warn Vassilisa. At the end of the second day and night, he arrived at the estate and found her about to enter the house.

"Mistress, you must flee!" he gasped. "Master Nickolai is in the dungeon and soldiers are coming to take you to court."

"What? Tell me all," she said. When he finished, she patted his arm. "Well done, Pyotr. You traveled fast and far. Now go. You need to eat and rest. I must think of what to do."

She walked back and forth in the garden, talking to herself as she paced. "Oh, Nickolai, your pride was always your weakness. What can I do to rescue you? How can I persuade the Prince to let you go?"

After some time Vassilisa had a plan. She ran into the house, calling her maidservants, "Katya, Sasha, come quick! Katya, find the robes the Tartar noble left behind when he visited my father years ago. Sasha, you must cut off my braids. And bring the dye we made from the walnut husks. Hurry! I must be ready before the soldiers come."

Some hours later what appeared to be a wealthy Tartar rode to meet the Prince's soldiers. Vassilisa's close-cropped, brown-dyed hair fit snugly beneath a fur-trimmed cap. "Is this where a young woman named Vassilisa is staying?" one of the soldiers asked Vassilisa.

"It is, but you are too late, soldiers. Vassilisa has flown. However, I am on my way to your Prince's court and wish to travel with you."

"Look at the golden threads adorning his caftan," one of the soldiers told the others. "Look at that fine horse he rides. He must be an important person. The son of a nobleman, at least. We must treat him with respect."

"A Tartar!" Prince Aleksei exclaimed when the soldiers escorted Vassilisa to him. "I did not know the Golden Horde was near here." He thought with fear of the large tribe of nomadic horsemen from Asia that had conquered vast territories. Why was this Tartar at his court, he wondered. Would his princedom be the next to be conquered? "You are welcome, young lord," the Prince added, looking at Vassilisa, who appeared to be a young lad, slim and well-favored.

"Call me Vassili," said Vassilisa. "I have come on a visit of friendship between our peoples." The Prince doubted her words, thinking that this Tartar had come to spy on his court. The Golden Horde had probably sent a lone young man so that he, Prince Aleksei, would not be suspicious. He had best be very polite to the Tartar. "You speak our language exceedingly well, and your eyes are blue, not black, like most of your countrymen's. Is your mother one of our people?"

"Yes," said Vassilisa. "But my heart is with my father's people." In truth, her heart was pounding so hard in her chest, she feared it might be heard.

"Come and eat and drink with us, young Vassili," said the Prince. "You must be weary from your travel."

"I accept your hospitality with thanks," said Vassilisa, and they entered the great hall.

"Uncle," whispered Princess Svetlana during the meal, tugging at the Prince's sleeve, "Uncle, that is not a man."

He shook her hand away. "Of course he is a man. He is a representative of the Golden Horde. Do not anger him."

Princess Svetlana persisted. "Uncle, that is a woman. See the graceful hands? See the soft cheeks? No beard will ever grow on those cheeks. Further, she does not look at me with admiration, the way all men do."

Prince Aleksei was afraid to anger the Tartar, but decided to test him. "Vassili, we have welcomed you to our court. Now it is time for amusement. Your people are noted for their archery. Would you care for a match against our champion, Ivan?"

"Gladly," said Vassilisa, thinking with relief of all the hours she had spent practicing archery with her brother and his friends instead of practicing her embroidery, as she should have been doing.

In the courtyard a target was set up. Vassilisa and Ivan both hit the center. It was moved farther away by ten paces. Again, both hit the center. It was moved farther away by twenty paces. Again, both hit the center.

"Let us try a harder target," said Vassilisa. She pointed to a large oak tree at the edge of the courtyard. "Do you see the branch that juts out to the right? There is an acorn at the end. Let us aim at that."

"I can barely see it," said Ivan. "No man could hit that." When the Prince glared at him, he nodded and took careful aim. The arrow fell short by a hand's width.

Vassilisa raised her bow and in a single quick movement let loose the arrow. It sped true to the mark and clipped the acorn from the branch. The crowd gazed long in stunned silence before raising a cheer for the marksmanship of the Tartar.

"You see? No woman could have done that," Prince Aleksei whispered to his niece.

"She is a woman. I know she is," insisted the Princess. "That took only skill, not a man's strength."

"Then let us test the Tartar again," said Prince Aleksei.

The Prince advanced to stand before Vassilisa. "Well done," he said. "Fine shooting. Tell me, young lord, are your people truly as splendid horsemen as they are reputed to be? Would you care for a race?"

"Gladly," said Vassilisa, grateful for all the hours she had spent riding with her brother and his friends instead of spinning wool, as she should have been doing. "What is the course?"

The Prince pointed to a tree far distant on the horizon. "Around that tree and back here."

"Oh, let it be more interesting," said Vassilisa. "Put up some obstacles to ride around."

"Agreed." The Prince directed soldiers to place posts to circle around and a fence to be jumped.

When the race began, the Prince's champion got a

better start and was slightly ahead. However, because she was lighter, Vassilisa did not have to slow her horse to make the maneuvers as he did. She was four horse's lengths ahead as she crossed the finish line. The crowd cheered loudly for the Tartar as she slid from her horse, flushed and laughing.

"Are you satisfied?" Prince Aleksei said to Princess Svetlana. "No woman can ride like that."

"Nevertheless, I am sure she is a woman," said the Princess. "Try one more test."

"All right. We will settle this for good. No woman can outthink me," said the Prince.

Prince Aleksei called Vassilisa to him. "Will you play chess with me, young Vassili? I have a fancy to see how your Tartar strategy will stand up to my good Russian skills."

"Gladly," said Vassilisa, "I have played since child-hood and welcome a match."

"Then shall we play for high stakes? If you lose, your Golden Horde will stay far from my city. If you win, you may ask one favor of me and I will grant it." The Prince shuddered after he had made the offer, realizing that the Tartar could exact a high price for the favor, but he could not now draw back honorably.

"It is a bet," said Vassilisa.

The chess set was lovely. The board itself was inlaid with ivory brought from afar and the chess pieces were of gold and silver set with precious gemstones. They played on and on. First the Prince was ahead, but then Vassilisa captured his bishop. Then Vassilisa was ahead until the Prince took her knight. The day grew dim so that it was hard to tell the gold pieces from the silver. Just as the Prince signaled for torches to be brought for light, Vassilisa cried out, "Checkmate! I have won!"

Prince Aleksei stared at the board. "You have beaten me." His face was pale. "What is the favor you will ask of me?"

"I will think and let you know," said Vassilisa.

That night at the great feast, Vassilisa sat with downcast eyes. "Are you displeased?" asked the Prince.

Vassilisa shrugged, ignoring Princess Svetlana, who sat pouting in the next chair. "I would have music to cheer me. I have heard of the skill of your musicians—let them play."

Every minstrel played, every singer sang, and every dancer danced. Vassilisa sat unsmiling. "Is it not to your liking?" asked the Prince.

"The wind howling across the plains in winter is more musical to me. I have a lyre with me, which came from a faraway land. No one in the Golden Horde can play a lyre and I wish to hear it played."

The Prince looked at his minstrels. All shook their heads. One officer spoke hesitantly from his seat, "Great Prince, remember the country lout who made such boasts about his village? He claimed he could play a lyre, if only he had one here."

"Bring him here," ordered the Prince.

Soon Nickolai stood before them, pale and hollow-cheeked. He looked in puzzlement at the Tartar. "No," he thought, "I am only dreaming. It can't be."

"Let him eat and drink," said Vassilisa, "and then he will play for us."

Nickolai ate and drank eagerly, for prison fare was tasteless and sparse. Then he picked up the lyre and knew it was his own. He smiled at Vassilisa and began to play.

He sang praises of his land, songs of verdant spring and golden autumn. He sang of honest sweat in the fields and the joy of the harvest. He sang of new birth and the love of a parent for a child. He sang of love and beauty and glory. Prince Aleksei, at first rigid with resentment, was soon caught under the spell. Nickolai sang and played with such sweetness and charm that everyone in the great hall was silent in wonder.

When Nickolai finished singing and playing, Vassilisa said, "This is the favor I have won of you. I wish you to give this man's freedom into my keeping."

"He is not my slave," said the Prince. "I cannot give him to you."

Vassilisa walked from her table and stood beside Nickolai. "He boasted that he could play better than any minstrel at court and he proved that he could. He boasted that his sister could outshoot and outride anyone at court and she proved she could. Will you not then release him, for he spoke the truth?"

Prince Aleksei looked down at the two standing before him. Two pairs of identical blue eyes looked back at him. For a moment the Prince was poised between anger and mirth. He chose mirth. He laughed until tears rolled down his cheeks. "How you tricked me! I truly believed you were a man, a young lad."

"Then was I not right?" asked Nickolai. "Is she not clever and skillful and beautiful?"

"You were right," said the Prince. "This time, at least, she was more clever than I. She even outplayed me in chess."

"But she is not beautiful," said Princess Svetlana with a purr. She tossed her glossy black tresses. "He said his sister is more beautiful than any at court, and that is not true."

Vassilisa clutched her cropped hair, dull and mottled brown. "Walnut stain," she stammered. "I did not want to look so much like Nickolai."

The Prince said gently, "Perhaps we should wait a few years to judge beauty, so that your braids can grow again. But now what we have here is more rare than beauty. We have a woman who is willing to sacrifice her beauty, at least temporarily, for the sake of someone she loves."

"Hah!" said Princess Svetlana as she flounced from the room.

"And now," said the Prince, "let us resume the feast. And you, Nickolai, will sit at my right hand, and you, Vassilisa, sit at my left. You must tell me more of this remarkable village of yours."

# Just a Girl

## AN ORIGINAL STORY BY BRENDA COX

**Arabic Words:**

*Halima* (pronounced "Hal-LEEM-ah"): means "gentle."

*Alif, Baa:* the first letters of the Arabic alphabet, like "A" and "B."

*Bab:* means "door."

*Ma' salaama* (pronounced "ma suh-LAM-uh"): means "good-bye."

*Madrasa* (pronounced "MUH-druh-suh"): means "school."

*Mafraj* (pronounced "MUH-fruj"): a Yemeni sitting room, with cushions along the walls.

Halima and her younger brother Ahmad scratched in the dirt with sticks. The tall houses of their Yemeni village blended into the mountainside. White-rimmed windows stared past the children down a giant staircase of terraced fields.

Ahmad wrote carefully in the sand. *"Baa, alif, baa: bab."*

Nine-year-old Halima tried to copy *bab,* the Arabic word for "door." Ahmad laughed at her squiggly letters. Their baby brother Yahya crawled to Ahmad and laughed too. "Baa-baa!" he shouted, poking the dirt with his chubby fingers. Halima moved to another spot and traced the letters again.

"There!" she said. "I wrote it."

"Well," said Ahmad, examining her writing, "it's not bad for a girl."

"I could write as well as you do if Father would let me go to school," retorted Halima. She brushed the dirt off her purple dress and embroidered pants.

"School! But you're just a girl. No girls from our village have ever gone to school. You have to stay home and help Mother. Anyway, the school is in a town a long way from here; it takes half an hour to walk there. A girl would get tired walking so far."

"I could do it."

"You'd get lost in the town. It's huge! There's a boy's school, a girl's school, a hospital, a mosque, and at least twenty shops."

"How do you find your way around then? How do you know what all those buildings are?"

"The hospital has a big red crescent on the front." Ahmad drew a quarter moon in the dust. "The mosque, where father goes to pray, has a big tall tower next to it, called a minaret. We hear the prayer call from the top of the minaret at noon." He drew a dome with a tower next to it. "The schools have big walls around them and signs that say *madrasa*. It's not so hard once you get used to it."

Halima sighed. She twisted the tassel of her black veil around her finger. "If only I could go to school and learn to read. I want to know so many things. I look at the mountains and dream about what might be beyond our village, but no one will tell me." Halima thought for a minute and then exclaimed, "I know!" She turned to Ahmad. "You've started school. Will you come home every day and tell me everything you've learned?"

"Maybe later," Ahmad said. "I'm going to play soccer with Ali now. *Ma' salaama!*" He waved good-bye.

Halima scooped up her baby brother, who was gurgling as he dug in the sand, and returned to the house. Somehow, someday, she'd prove she wasn't "just a girl"!

The next morning Halima's mother announced,

"Your father and I are going to my parents' village today with your cousins. Do the housework and keep baby Yahya out of trouble."

"I'll be careful, Mama," Halima promised.

When everyone had gone, Halima did her morning chores. She went into the *mafraj* room where her parents sat with friends in the afternoons and where the children slept at night. She carefully arranged the big cushions all around the edge of the room and swept the carpet. Then she went outside and fed the cow, sheep, and chickens. She gathered eggs and brought in firewood.

After baking bread for lunch, Halima went down the hill to fetch water. She balanced a water jar on her head, with Yahya on her hip, and traced her way up to the house without spilling a drop.

At the front door she sat down to rest. Thankful for his freedom, Yahya crawled off to explore some rocks nearby.

Suddenly he began screaming. Halima caught her breath. She saw a big brown scorpion on Yahya's arm. Swallowing her fear, Halima brushed off the ugly creature and smashed it with a rock.

She picked up the baby and tried to comfort him,

but it was no use. He screamed louder with pain. She could see the tiny stinger in his arm. Halima tried to pull it out, but the stinger only went in deeper.

What could she do? Last year a baby in her village died of a scorpion sting!

All her relatives had left in the village's only car. Her brothers were at school. The nearest doctor was in town. She would have to take the baby there herself. She knew where the road was; surely she would just have to follow it. But how would her parents know where she had gone?

Halima picked up the stick she used for "lessons" with Ahmad. In the dirt she drew pictures of a baby and a scorpion with its tail pointing toward the baby. How could she show the town? The closest hospital was in town; that would be easy to draw, since Ahmad had shown her how. Halima drew a big crescent, and showed a girl walking toward it. She hoped her parents would understand her message.

She thought for a moment about the baby who was stung last year. What did his father say? When they got to the hospital, the doctor had asked to see the scorpion so they'd know how to treat the baby. Halima would have to bring the scorpion with her.

Shuddering, she wrapped the dead creature in a cloth and tied it to the sash of her dress.

Halima carried her crying brother back down the steep path, past the water tank, stumbling over stones. Thorns caught at her pants and scratched her sandaled feet. Finally she reached the paved road to town. She raced along it until she was almost exhausted. Yahya, whimpering now, felt heavier and heavier.

But Halima did not stop; she hurried on and on. She passed the school, where children were shouting and laughing in the yard, and the mosque, with its tall minaret broadcasting the morning call to prayer. Finally she saw a white building. A red crescent moon was painted on the wall: surely it was the hospital! Thankfully, Halima stumbled through the door.

Late that evening, Halima's father found her nearly asleep by Yahya's hospital bed.

"She's a brave girl, and intelligent too," Halima heard the doctor whisper to her father. "She even brought the scorpion so we knew exactly how to treat the baby. It was a serious sting. The little boy might have died if she hadn't brought him here so quickly."

Her father watched Halima and his peacefully sleeping son for a while. At last he said, "I saw your message and came right away. Halima, I'm proud of you. You'll be a good mother someday."

"I knew how to find the hospital because Ahmad taught me its sign," Halima told him. "I wish I could learn to read the word for hospital, though, and lots of other words!"

"Is that right?" asked her father thoughtfully. "Well, how would you like to be the first girl from our village ever to go to school?"

"Oh, Father!" Halima exclaimed, flinging her arms around him.

Soon Halima was the happiest, hardest-working girl in first grade.

# The Clever Daughter-in-Law

ADAPTED BY BRUCE LANSKY
FROM CHINESE FOLKLORE

The evening sun streamed through the tea house window as Old Chang sipped hot tea and counted his blessings. If you looked carefully, you could see a smile on his face as he silently expressed gratitude for a trustworthy wife, a close-knit family, and a successful tea house that provided a comfortable living for them all.

But although Old Chang had succeeded in building a successful business, he had not yet figured out a way to retire. He still worked from dawn to dark most days, because whenever he let one of his three sons run the tea house, something would go wrong.

His eldest son was impractical. He could not carry out the simplest task without making a mess of it. His middle son was quick-tempered—not the kind of person who could get along with others. His youngest son was good-natured, but lazy. He was more likely to be late to work than on time. Old Chang could not turn his business over to any of his sons. So, he would have to find someone else.

Old Chang's two older sons were married, but their wives had not shown much interest in the tea house. Old Chang wondered whether either of them might have the talent to manage it some day. But how could he find out? He decided to discuss the matter with his wife and trusted advisor, Jiao Peng.

"Before you offer them responsibility," she suggested, "why not test them to see how clever they are?"

"I would be very happy if I discovered that they were half as clever as you," Old Chang responded. Then he summoned his daughters-in-law.

The young women stood before the head of the household with worried expressions on their faces and wondered why they had been called. Perhaps, they thought, they had done something to displease Old Chang. But instead of a reprimand, Old Chang surprised them. "Neither of you have been home to visit your parents for quite a while," he told them. "Spring is a beautiful time of year to travel. Perhaps you would like to go home to see your parents?"

Mei Ling, the older daughter-in-law, said, "Thank you, Honorable Father. You are very thoughtful."

Jing Wei, the younger daughter-in-law, said, "I have not seen my parents for more than a year. I appreciate your kind offer."

As the young women were leaving the room, Old Chang called out, "One more thing. A small favor, if you don't mind..."

They stopped and turned around, "Yes, Honorable Father?" Mei Ling asked.

"Mei Ling, as a special favor, would you please bring back a fire wrapped in paper?"

"Of course, Honorable Father," Mei Ling responded dutifully.

"And, Jing Wei, I have a favor to ask of you as well. Would you please bring me the wind's song?"

"With pleasure, Honorable Father," said Jing Wei, bowing.

Puzzled, the two young women turned and left the room. They packed quickly, took leave of their husbands, and were soon on their way. It was a bright spring day—perfect for traveling. As they walked, they talked. And what they talked about were the unusual requests Old Chang had made.

"What on earth do you suppose he meant by a 'fire wrapped in paper'?" asked Mei Ling.

"I have no idea," Jing Wei answered. "Can you help me figure out what he meant by 'wind's song'?"

"I don't have a clue," answered Mei Ling. "But I do know this. If we don't bring back whatever it was that he requested, we will be in deep trouble."

The more they talked, the slower they walked. Soon they had stopped walking altogether and were sitting at the table of an inn near the village, trying to figure out Old Chang's riddles.

A waitress with long pigtails stopped to take their order. "What would you like?" she asked.

Without thinking, the young women blurted out what was on their minds:

"I'd like a fire wrapped in paper," Mei Ling answered.

"I'd like the wind's song," said Jing Wei.

"I'm sorry, but we don't sell lanterns or wind chimes here. Try the market in Shanghai. Now, what would you like to eat?" the waitress asked.

Mei Ling's mouth dropped open. "Thank you so very, very much!" she exclaimed. She reached into her purse and pulled out a silver coin, which she put on the table. "You don't know how much you've helped me. Suddenly, I'm not hungry."

"Come to think of it, I'm not hungry either," echoed Jing Wei as she dropped a silver coin on the table. "Thank you, from the bottom of my heart."

Mei Ling and Jing Wei left the inn without eating a bite. Smiling, they began the long journey towards their parents' homes at a brisk pace.

When they returned the following week, the first thing that Mei Ling and Jing Wei did was visit Old Chang. First Mei Ling handed him a beautifully wrapped gift. "Here is the fire wrapped in paper you requested," she said, bowing. "I hope you like it."

When Old Chang unwrapped the paper lantern, his eyes opened wide with surprise. "Thank you so much!" he exclaimed.

Then it was Jing Wei's turn to hand him a wrapped gift. "I brought you the wind's song. I hope it pleases you."

When Old Chang had unwrapped the wind chimes made of oyster shells, the surprise on his face was even greater.

"I could not be more delighted," he said. "I congratulate you on solving the riddles." Both daughters-in-law smiled proudly. "Now tell me, how did you do it?" he added.

"Well, to tell the truth," began Mei Ling, "we did have a little help."

"Actually, we were quite confused until we met a waitress with pigtails at the inn on the edge of town," added Jing Wei.

"Hmmm," thought Old Chang as his daughters-in-law left the room. "Perhaps Mei Ling and Jing Wei are not clever enough to manage the tea house without me, but they may have found someone who can. I must meet this waitress for myself."

That evening, Old Chang and his wife, Jiao Peng, went out to dine at the inn. Old Chang spotted a slender young woman with pigtails who was waiting on several tables at the same time—and managing to keep all the diners happy.

As soon as Old Chang and Jiao Peng seemed ready

to order, the waitress was standing at their table with a big smile. "What would you like?" she asked.

"I'd like a rainbow in a stone," he answered.

"I'm sorry, but all the pearls have been removed from our oysters—so you don't break a tooth. How many oysters would you like?"

Old Chang was impressed by her cleverness. "What is your name?"

"I am called Jin Chen."

"Ah, Golden Treasure," he said. "You are well named." He and Madame Chang ordered dinner and were pleased by Jin Chen's service.

The next day, Old Chang asked a matchmaker to arrange a marriage between Jin Chen and his third son, Tai Shan.

"My job may not be an easy one. No offense intended," the matchmaker said, "but Tai Shan is known throughout the village as a young man who would rather do anything than work. Jin Chen's father may not approve of the marriage."

Old Chang said, "Tell Jin Chen's father that his daughter will be marrying into a wealthy family, so she will never have to worry about money. Offer him as many gifts as it will take to gain his approval."

And that is exactly what the matchmaker did. But Jin Chen's father was very wise. He told the matchmaker that he would withhold his approval until after Jin Chen had met Tai Shan. Luckily for Old Chang, the meeting went well. Tai Shan admired Jin Chen's wit. And Jin Chen enjoyed Tai Shan's company. Jin Chen's father gave his approval.

The marriage worked out much better than Old Chang could have ever predicted. Jin Chen did such a good job in the tea house, he appointed her to manage it. Soon, she had made the tea house the most popular gathering place in the village. Following her good example, Tai Shan began showing up at work on time. They worked well together and enjoyed each other's company.

After turning the tea house over to Jin Chen, Old Chang was finally able to retire and spend time in his garden at home with his wife.

One evening, while enjoying a birthday celebration with his family in the tea house, he stood up at his table and made a toast: "Surely I am the luckiest man alive to have such a fine wife and family and to be able to enjoy the fruits of a lifetime of hard work."

Unfortunately, the local prefect was seated at a table nearby. He overheard Old Chang's toast and said, "I could not help but overhear your boastful remark. See me in my office tomorrow morning."

The next morning Old Chang went to the prefect's office, not knowing what to expect. The self-righteous prefect began lecturing him. "How dare you boast publicly about being 'the luckiest man alive.' You need to be taught a lesson in humility. Let us see how lucky you really are. I will give you three tasks to perform: First, bring me a rooster that can lay eggs. Second, bring me enough silk to cover the sky. Third, bring me enough tea to fill the ocean."

Old Chang was in a state of shock. He stammered, "But those tasks are impossible, Your Honor."

The angry prefect interrupted, "I will give you three days to complete your tasks. If you fail, you will be severely punished."

Old Chang bowed and mumbled, "As you wish, Your Honor." Then he left the prefect's office, trembling. His world was about to crumble. Instead of enjoying his golden years in prosperity he would be publicly ridiculed and would have to live out his life in shame.

When he got home, his wife, Jiao Peng, noticed that there were worry lines on his face instead of his usual smile. She also noticed that he paced nervously back and forth instead of working in the garden. And that night, she heard him tossing and turning in his bed instead of falling right to sleep.

Finally, Jiao Peng asked, "What is troubling you? You have not been your normal cheerful self all day."

After keeping his thoughts to himself, the words came tumbling out of Old Chang's mouth. He told her what had happened at the prefect's office. At the end of his story he moaned, "Everything I've worked so hard for my whole life may be lost."

Jiao Peng spoke wisely, "Do not despair. Tomorrow we will consult our clever daughter-in-law. Perhaps she can help."

"I hope you are right," replied Old Chang glumly.

"Now, try to get some sleep. You will have to think clearly tomorrow," his wife suggested.

The next morning Old Chang described to Jin Chen what the prefect had said and then added, "He has asked me to do what no man can do. If I do not carry out his orders, I will be humiliated. I can see no way out of this terrible predicament."

"Don't worry, Honorable Father," Jin Chen replied. "Tomorrow I shall visit the prefect on your behalf. Perhaps I can convince him to be lenient with you."

"Thank you, Jin Chen. I wish you luck."

The next day Jin Chen arrived at the prefect's office carrying a ruler and a ladle.

"What are you doing here?" asked the prefect gruffly.

"I am Jin Chen, daughter-in-law of Old Chang," she began.

The prefect cut her off before she could say another word. "Where is Old Chang? He is supposed to report to me today about the three tasks I asked him to do."

"I am sorry to inform you that he could not be here. You see, he is home giving birth to a baby."

"You must be crazy!" shouted the prefect. "How can a man give birth to a baby?"

"With all due respect, Your Honor, if you don't believe that a man can give birth to a baby, then surely you don't believe that a rooster can lay an egg. So there's no point in asking Old Chang to bring you one," Jin Chen retorted.

The prefect was flustered, but tried to remain calm.

"Very well," he continued, "have you brought enough silk to cover the sky?"

"Old Chang has plenty of silk, Your Honor. But

Old Chang is not sure exactly how much silk you will require. So, I have brought you a ruler. As soon as you provide me with the exact measurements of the sky, Old Chang will be happy to bring you the proper amount of silk."

"Forget the silk," the annoyed prefect snapped. "Have you brought enough tea to fill up the ocean?"

"Old Chang has lots of tea, Your Honor," answered Jin Chen politely. "But Old Chang cannot fill up the ocean with tea until the ocean is empty. So, I have brought you a ladle. As soon as you empty the ocean, Old Chang will be happy to bring you enough tea to fill it back up."

The prefect was beside himself with anger. He had been outwitted by a young woman with pigtails. After Jin Chen had left his office, the prefect began to think about her. Upon reflection, he had to agree with Old Chang. With a clever daughter-in-law like Jin Chen, surely Old Chang was the luckiest man alive.

# Peggy's Magic Egg

## ADAPTED BY STEPHEN MOOSER
## FROM AN IRISH FOLKTALE

Once, not so long ago, in a land everyone now calls Ireland lived a poor girl named Peggy O'Neil and her chicken Penny. Though they were as poor as the stones that dotted their tiny farm, they were rich in other ways. Together they shared the sky, the sunlight, and the sparkling waters of the little river that ran through their land. Peggy harvested corn in the fall so that she and Penny would have food through the year, and Penny always provided an egg each day, which kept Peggy well-fed and happy.

And happy they were, which is something that no one ever said about Peggy's neighbors, Riley and Wiley. The two lived together just up the river on a huge, poorly kept farm. Riley was a sour-tempered man whose face was always decorated with a scowl. Wiley was nearly as unpleasant. However, unlike his brother, his face always displayed a grin. This smile, though, was as false as the words that flowed in torrents from his lips. He was, in fact, quite a nasty fellow. Over the years his lies and empty promises had cheated many of his neighbors out of their farms. Most of these poor people now lived in the city where they spent their days begging for food to feed their hungry families.

Peggy's was the one farm that Riley and Wiley could not seem to get their greedy hands on.

One day the two evil neighbors knocked on Peggy's door. "Taking care of a farm all by yourself must be hard work," said Wiley, a fat smile plastered across his face. "Why don't you sell us your place and retire. You deserve a nice vacation."

"That's a very kind thought," said Peggy, not believing him for a moment. "But nothing you say could ever make me sell my beautiful home. Maybe you were able to cheat my neighbors out of their land, but you're not going to be able to cheat me."

"What ever are you talking about?" asked Wiley, smiling innocently. "My brother and I would never cheat anyone."

"Begone!" said Peggy, waving them away with the back of her hand. "I'll not sell. Ever!"

"Have you no brains, girl?" grumbled Riley. He sniffled and wiped his runny nose on the sleeve of his dirty jacket. Then he reached into his pocket and pulled out a shiny gold piece. "Take it! Wouldn't you rather be rich than poor?"

"I *am* rich," said Peggy, her blue eyes sparkling as bright as the warm summer day. "I have all that I need—a fine little farmhouse, a field of sweet corn, and the friendship of the best little hen in the world, Penny."

"She's as stubborn as an old mule," grumbled Riley after Peggy had slammed the door. He kicked over a potted plant with one of his big feet. "Face it, Wiley, we'll never get our hands on her land."

"Don't be so certain," said Wiley, a plan percolating in his brain. "She says she's happy today, but, I wonder, will she be happy tomorrow?"

Riley tilted his head, "What do you mean?"

"You'll see," said Wiley, giving his brother a fat wink. "I've got a plan that's going to turn her into the saddest girl in the world."

"Now that is a lovely thought," said Riley.

"I promise. By tomorrow she'll be so miserable she'll be begging us to take her land."

And, for once, even Riley smiled.

That night, long after midnight, when darkness lay upon the land like a thick wool blanket and even the owls were snoring in their nests, Riley and Wiley snuck into Peggy's barn, threw a sack over Penny's head, and stole her away.

In the morning when Peggy went out to the barn she found a solitary egg sitting in Penny's nest, but not a sign of the one who had laid it.

"Penny! Penny!" she cried, frantically running about the farm. "My dear, dear friend. Where are you?"

When Penny did not come running, Peggy immediately feared the worst.

"An evil fox must have eaten her," she sobbed, tears flooding down her pink cheeks. "My best friend ever. Gone!"

Peggy sat down on her porch and buried her head in her hands. Her grief was so great that it seemed as if she might shake apart with sobs.

"There will never be another Penny," she cried. "Alas, this farm is now the loneliest place on earth."

"Trust me. It will only get lonelier," came a familiar voice. Peggy sniffled and raised her head. It was Wiley. Behind him, his face as sour as a rotten lemon, was Riley.

"Why suffer anymore?" said Riley. "Go as far from here as you can."

Peggy dried her tears, then narrowed her eyes and rubbed her chin. In a few short moments she realized that perhaps a fox wasn't responsible for her hen's disappearance after all.

"We'll buy your farm and then you won't have to stay here all alone," said Wiley with a sly smile. "It's the least we can do in your time of need."

"You're very kind," said Peggy, a plan now forming in her own head. "Without Penny's magic eggs I'd never be able to afford to stay."

"Magic eggs?" said Riley, raising an eyebrow as he rubbed at his stubbly chin.

"Worth their weight in gold," said Peggy. "Poor me. Only one remains in the barn. After the king pays me for it, perhaps it would be best to sell the farm."

"An excellent idea," said Wiley. Then off the two

went, certain that by the end of the week Peggy's land would be theirs.

"Do you really think that chicken's eggs are magic?" asked Riley as they shuffled down the dusty road.

"Of course not, you cabbagehead," said Wiley, wondering how he could be a brother to such a fool. "There's no such thing as an egg worth its weight in gold."

As soon as Riley and Wiley were out of sight, Peggy jumped up and ran to the barn. Penny's last egg still lay in the nest.

"You may be gone, my dear, dear friend," said Peggy. "But together we can still outwit those thick-headed neighbors of mine."

Peggy took the egg into the kitchen, carefully cut off one end, and emptied the shell. When the shell had dried, she filled it with all the coins she could find in her house, making sure not to crack the shell. Then she glued the egg back up and went off to see the king.

When she got to the castle, she took a deep breath and knocked on the big wooden door.

"What do you want, little girl?" barked the page who opened the door.

"My name is Peggy O'Neil and I have come to sell the king an egg," said Peggy loudly.

"Go away!" said the page, starting to close the door. "We have all the eggs we need."

"Ah, but this is a special egg, a magic egg," said Peggy, keeping the door open with her foot. "It's worth its weight in gold."

"Nonsense!" scoffed the page, but just before he could shoo her away, the king himself called out.

"Let young Peggy O'Neil in," he commanded. "Let me see what kind of egg could be worth its weight in gold."

And so Peggy was allowed to enter the castle. The king, a huge, bearded man dressed in his fine purple robes, was seated on his throne.

"Show me this magical egg," he demanded.

Peggy nervously approached the king, her legs quivering, her heart pounding.

"Here it is," she said as she held the egg over the king's lap, being careful to hide the glued seam. "Now watch!"

And with that she broke the egg in two and out poured a torrent of coins.

The king clapped his hands with joy for he had never seen such a marvelous thing. Then he had his page fetch Peggy a fistful of gold coins.

"And I thought I'd seen everything there was to

see," said the king, still shaking his head in amazement. He patted Peggy on the shoulder. "I must show my royal court your wondrous eggs. Please, bring me some more and I promise that you'll be richly rewarded."

"Alas, someone has stolen my magic hen," said Peggy, wiping a pretend tear from her eye. "I fear she is as heartbroken as I and may never again lay a magic egg."

The king's smile turned at once into a dark scowl. "I'll not tolerate thieves in my kingdom! I'll order my knights to comb the countryside and bring the scoundrels to the castle."

"That may not be necessary," said Peggy. "I have a feeling they may soon come to the castle on their own, trying to sell the eggs."

"We'll watch for them then," said the king, bidding Peggy good-bye. "And thank you again for such a marvelous treat."

On the way back to the farm, Peggy saw Wiley and Riley sitting beneath a big oak being their usual lazy selves.

"Peggy!" called out Wiley. He poked Riley in the ribs and winked. "Did the king give you a pile of gold for your magic egg?"

The two of them laughed, but their silly giggles

stopped soon enough when Peggy showed them the king's gold.

"He gave you all of that for a single egg?" gasped Riley.

"Yes," said Peggy, "and he would have given me three times as much if I'd had three eggs. Alas, my hen has been eaten by a fox so I have no more eggs for the king."

Riley and Wiley exchanged a greedy look. "He'd like more eggs, you say?" asked Riley.

"Those were his very words," said Peggy. She sighed.

Before she could say another word, Riley and Wiley were off down the road, hurrying as fast as their fat legs could carry them to where they had hidden Penny away in the coop.

Wasting no time, Riley and Wiley took the egg Penny had laid that morning and hurried to the castle.

"Your Majesty, we have come to present you with a magic egg," said Wiley as the page showed them into the throne room.

"In exchange for its weight in gold, of course," said Riley, rubbing his hands together greedily.

The king motioned for Riley and Wiley to approach the throne with the egg. Then he called the royal court to come see the egg with coins for a yolk. And he called his guards too.

"Watch these two," he whispered. "I'm guessing they're the thieves Peggy warned us about."

"Crack it open," said the king as Wiley held out the egg.

"But...but Your Majesty," stammered Wiley. "I'm holding it over your lap. Do you want me to open it over the royal robes?"

"Of course!" commanded the king. "My robe has nothing to fear from a few coins."

"Coins?" said Wiley. He winced and cracked open the egg and, as he did, the sticky contents poured out onto the king's precious robe.

The royal court gasped.

"What is the meaning of this?" thundered the king, pointing to his dripping, sticky, ruined robe.

For the moment Riley and Wiley were stunned speechless, their mouths flopped open like oven doors.

"Speak up! Are you the thieves who took poor Peggy's hen?" demanded the king.

An instant later Riley and Wiley were blaming each other for the foul fowl deed. By the time they were done they had convicted each other many times over. The king could have easily tossed them into his dungeon for the crime. But, being a relatively kindly fellow, all he did was banish them from the kingdom forever.

Happy to escape with their lives, Riley and Wiley ran from the castle and, for all anyone knows, they are running still.

Early the next day Peggy went to Riley and Wiley's abandoned farm and found Penny.

"Oh, how I missed you," she cried, sweeping the hen into her arms. "Your eggs not only saved my farm, they saved you as well."

Penny clucked in reply and, though she couldn't say so in words, her eyes told Peggy how much she had been missed and loved.

As is the case in stories such as these, Peggy and Penny lived to a ripe old age, happily sharing their lives together on the beautiful little farm.

And what of the farm once owned by Riley and Wiley? Peggy, with the king's blessing, returned most of it to the people Riley and Wiley had cheated. The rest was made into a park, so that everyone in the kingdom could enjoy the outdoors and appreciate that wealth came in many forms and that those who had the sky, the sunlight, and sparkling waters, as well as true friends, were really the richest of all.

# AUTHOR BIOGRAPHIES

**Brenda S. Cox** is an American who has lived in the Middle Eastern country of Yemen for twelve years. She has also lived in Jordan and the United Arab Emirates. Brenda speaks Arabic and is friends with many special Yemeni girls (most of whom live in the city and have the privilege of attending school). She has a degree in chemical engineering from Georgia Technical College, but is now fully occupied with writing and with homeschooling her four children. Brenda loves languages and is the author of *Who Talks Funny? A Book about Languages for Kids,* published by Linnet Books, 1995. Her story, "Just a Girl," is original.

**Douglas C. Dosson** is an attorney in Roscommon, Michigan, but has a significant background in writing. A member of the Society of Children's Book Writers and Illustrators since 1987, Doug has written more than fifty children's stories, which he often shares with numerous elementary schools in northern Michigan. His efforts earned him the SCBWI-MI Memorial Award in 1995. Since many of his stories are written for his daughter, Lisa, it is not unusual that his main character is a little girl, as is the case with "Cody's Wooden Whistle."

**Lois Greiman** is an award-winning novelist with five books to her credit. Born a North Dakota farm girl, she finds she most enjoys living vicariously through her fictional characters. Lois lives with her veterinarian husband, their three children, and a menagerie of pets on a small horse farm in Dayton, Minnesota.

**Bruce Lansky** enjoys writing stories and performing them as plays at school assemblies, teacher conferences, and bookstores. He also writes children's poetry. *Poetry Party* is a collection of his funniest poems; *The New Adventures of Mother Goose* is a collection of his funniest nursery rhymes. Before he started to write children's books, Lansky wrote humorous books for parents and baby name books. He has two grown children and currently lives with his computer near a beautiful lake in Minnesota. Of his stories, "Liza and the Lost Letter" is original, and "The Clever Daughter-in-Law" and "Kim's Surprise Witness" are adapted from Chinese folklore.

**Joanne Mitchell** lives in Rochester, New York, with her husband. Their two sons are both college students. Joanne graduated from MIT with a Ph.D. in chemistry and now works as a technical writer. She has had short stories published in *Isaac Asimov's Science Fiction Magazine* and in *Aboriginal Science Fiction Magazine*. In addition to reading and writing, Joanne enjoys baking bread, hiking, canoeing, and sea kayaking. She also practices t'ai chi every day. Her story, "Vassilisa the Wise," is based on a Russian folk tale.

**Stephen Mooser** has written more than fifty books for children, ranging from picture books, such as *The Ghost with the Halloween Hiccups* (Avon), to nonfiction, such as *Into the Unknown: Nine Astounding Stories* (Macmillan), to novels, such as *Elvis Is Back and He's in the Sixth Grade!* (Dell), as well as two chapter-book series for Dell, *The Creepy Creature* books and the *All-Star Meatballs* books. A former filmmaker and treasure hunter, Stephen's adventures have made their way into many of his books. Currently President of the Society of Children's Book Writers and Illustrators, he has two children, Chelsea and Bryn, and lives in Los Angeles, California. His story, "Peggy's Magic Egg," is adapted from an Irish folktale.

**Anne Schraff** currently lives in Spring Valley, California. As a small child, Anne traveled all over America with her brother and widowed mother. Her mother's courage served as a shining example that encouraged Anne to pursue her dream of becoming a writer. As she watched her mother pull their trailer over the mountains, change tires, and do carpentry and electrical work on their cabin, Anne knew that just as her mom let nothing stand in her way, so would nothing ever stop her either. Her stories, "Adrianna's Chickens" and "Jamila and the Lion," are original.

## *The Girls to the Rescue Series*
Edited by Bruce Lansky

Here are seven collections of stories featuring heroic, clever, and determined girls from around the world. Each book contains tales about girls such as Emily, who helps a runaway slave and her baby reach safety and freedom, and Kamala, a Punjabi girl who outsmarts a pack of thieves. This series for girls ages 7 to 13 has received critical acclaim and raves from mothers and daughters alike.

## *Young Marian's Adventures in Sherwood Forest*
**A Girls to the Rescue novel**
Written by Stephen Mooser; Edited by Bruce Lansky

The Sheriff of Nottingham learned the hard way. Don't mess with Maid Marian! Thirteen-year-old Maid Marian is on her first adventure with young Robin of Loxley. The Sheriff of Nottingham has thrown Marian's father into the dungeon, and only Marian can save her father from the hangman's noose.

## *Newfangled Fairy Tales Series*
Edited by Bruce Lansky

This is a delightful fairy tale series with new twists on old stories and themes, including a beautiful princess who is put to sleep for 100 years because she is so cranky. And Michelle, who desperately wants to be a princess until her wish comes true and she discovers what a pain royal life can be; and Hansel, who is so obsessed with candy that he steals Gretel's piggy bank and runs off to the Old Witch's Candy Factory. This series for boys & girls ages 7 to 13.

We offer many more titles written to delight, inform, and entertain. To browse our full selection of titles, visit our web site at:

# www.meadowbrookpress.com

For quantity discounts, please call: 1-800-338-2232

### Meadowbrook Press